Little Sticker Dolly Dressing
Costume Parade

Written by Fiona Watt

Illustrated by Lizzie Mackay

Designed by Johanna Furst

Additional design Antonia Mille[r]

Contents

Join the parade!

It's carnival time, and Cara and Aimee are taking part in a street parade. They are dressed in outfits decorated with lots of leaves and bright tropical flowers.

Cara

Aimee

Dress the dolls in clothes for the parade,
then decorate the pages with
the rest of the stickers.

Anya

Watery world

Anya and Lily have joined the parade, dressed as
mermaids. They're both wearing headdresses made from
seashells and outfits that look like mermaids' tails.

Lily

Millie

6

Fire and Ice

Millie's clothes and headdress are covered in patterns that look like swirling flames, while Nadia's outfit is decorated with shiny snowflakes and twinkling crystals.

Nadia

Alice

Lottie

Venetian masks

Dressed in long ballgowns, Alice and Lottie
are hiding their faces behind traditional masks,
like those from the famous carnival in Venice.

Ella

Clowning around

Ella and Kayla are dressed as circus clowns.
They've put on brightly patterned clothes and
had their faces painted too.

Kayla

11

Lexie

Samba

Lexie and Zara are dancing to the lively rhythm of drums as they take part in the costume parade. They're shaking wooden maracas in time to the beat of the music.

Zara

13

Nina

14

Ruby

Springtime

Nina and Ruby are dressed in outfits inspired by nature.
Nina's wearing a headdress made from fresh flowers,
twigs and leaves, while Ruby's hat looks
like a giant upside-down flower.

Buzz and flutter

Freya and Jade are following the group of flowers in the parade. Freya's dressed as a bee, in a yellow and black striped top. Jade is wearing a mask and has big butterfly wings tied to her shoulders.

Freya

Jade

Feathery friends

With their arms stretched out, Amelie and Maddie flap their arms in time to the beat of the lively music.

Amelie

Maddie

19

Keira

Lara

Fairytale princesses

Keira and Lara are dressed as princesses.
Keira's wearing a tall wig, decorated with flowers
and feathers. Lara's holding the hem of her skirt
as she walks elegantly in the parade.

Lola

Woodland folk

Lola's dressed as a fairy queen.
She's wearing a wide-sleeved top and
a long flowing skirt. Asha's dressed like a pixie,
with a headdress made of leaves.

Asha

23

Fireworks

Maya is ready for bed. The parade is over but the
celebrations continue with a spectacular firework display.

Join the parade
Pages 2-3

Cara's headdress

Cara's outfit

Aimee's headdress

Flowers for Cara's ankles

Aimee's top and skirt

Flowers for Aimee's ankles

Watery world
Pages 4-5

A string of shells for Anya to hold

Anya's headdress

Anya's outfit

Anya's shoes

Lily's headdress and top

A shell for Lily to hold

Lily's shoes

Fire and Ice
Pages 6-7

Put Millie's skirt on before her top.

Millie's headdress

Millie's boots

Nadia's headdress

Nadia's outfit

Venetian masks
Pages 8-9

A sparkler for
Alice to hold

Alice's mask

Put Alice's
skirt on before
her top.

Lottie's mask

Lottie's
glove

Lottie's sparkler

Put Lottie's skirt
on before her top.

Clowning around
Pages 10-11

Ella's clown nose and hat

Kayla's nose and hat

Kayla's outfit

Ella's outfit

Samba
Pages 12-13

Lexie's top

Zara's top and skirt

Lexie's headdress

Lexie's skirt

Zara's headdress

Springtime
Pages 14–15

Nina's headdress

Nina's outfit

Ruby's hat

Ruby's flower basket

Ruby's outfit

Buzz and flutter
Pages 16–17

Freya's wings

Freya's outfit

A mask and bag for Freya to hold

Jade's mask

Jade's wings

Jade's dress

Feathery friends
Pages 18-19

Feathers for Amelie's hair

Amelie's wings

Amelie's outfit

Put Maddie's skirt on before her top.

Maddie's mask

Maddie's outfit

Fairytale princesses
Pages 20-21

Put the dolls' shoes on first, before dressing them.

Keira's wig

Put Keira's skirt on before her top.

Keira's skirt and shoes

Lara's top

Keira's fan

A mirror and crowns for the background

Lara's skirt

Woodland folk
Pages 22-23

Lola's tiara

Put Lola's skirt on before her top.

Asha's headdress

A bag of fairy dust

Asha's outfit

Decorate the background with the fireworks and the carnival mask.

Fireworks
Page 24